PUFFIN BOOKS

Geraldine Gets Lucky

Also by Robert Leeson in Puffin

NEVER KISS FROGS

For older readers

THE DOG WHO CHANGED THE WORLD
TOM'S PRIVATE WAR

Other titles in the First Young Puffin series

BEAR'S BAD MOOD John Prater
BELLA AT THE BALLET Brian Ball
BLESSU Dick King-Smith
BUBBLEGUM BOTHER Wendy Smith
THE DAY THE SMELLS WENT WRONG Catherine Sefton
THE DAY WE BRIGHTENED UP THE SCHOOL Mick Gowar
DIZ AND THE BIG FAT BURGLAR Margaret Stuart Barry
DUMPLING Dick King-Smith
ERIC'S ELEPHANT ON HOLIDAY John Gatehouse
FETCH THE SLIPPER Sheila Lavelle
GOODNIGHT, MONSTER Carolyn Dinan
HAPPY CHRISTMAS, RITA! Hilda Offen
HARRY'S AUNT Sheila Lavelle
HOP IT, DUGGY DOG! Brian Ball
THE INCREDIBLE SHRINKING HIPPO Stephanie Baudet
RAJ IN CHARGE Andrew and Diana Davies
RITA THE RESCUER Hilda Offen
THE ROMANTIC GIANT Kaye Umansky
SOS FOR RITA Hilda Offen
WHAT STELLA SAW Wendy Smith

Geraldine Gets Lucky

Robert Leeson

Illustrated by
Susie Poole

PUFFIN BOOKS

For Marius and Sandra

The text of this story first appeared as *The Frog Who Went a-Wooing* in *Puffin Flight* magazine, which is a publication of the Puffin Book Club.

PUFFIN BOOKS

Published by the Penguin Group
Penguin Books Ltd, 27 Wrights Lane, London W8 5TZ, England
Penguin Books USA Inc., 375 Hudson Street, New York, New York 10014, USA
Penguin Books Australia Ltd, Ringwood, Victoria, Australia
Penguin Books Canada Ltd, 10 Alcorn Avenue, Toronto, Ontario, Canada M4V 3B2
Penguin Books (NZ) Ltd, 182–190 Wairau Road, Auckland 10, New Zealand

Penguin Books Ltd, Registered Offices: Harmondsworth, Middlesex, England

First published by Hamish Hamilton Ltd 1995
Published in Puffin Books 1997
1 3 5 7 9 10 8 6 4 2

Filmset in Plantin

Made and printed in Hong Kong by Imago Publishing Limited

Once upon a time there was a frog, named Geraldine. She lived in a meadow pond with her parents and hundreds of brothers and sisters, uncles, aunts and cousins.

She was lean, green and not at all mean. She was like all the other frogs in the pond, but with one difference.

Geraldine had a dream. She was sure that one fine day she would meet a prince, a handsome prince, with a crown and a castle. He would look at her, he would bend down, pick her up, kiss her and she would turn into a princess. The trumpets would sound, they would be married and live happily ever after.

But when she told the other frogs, they all said, "You don't believe that old fairy story, do you?"

And they laughed so much they fell off their lily pads.

But her mother didn't think it was funny at all.

"What do you want to turn into a princess for?" she asked. "Humans look terrible, a funny colour, small mouths and hair all over the place. Why can't you fall in love with a nice frog with beautiful bulging eyes, a slippery green skin and a gorgeous big mouth, someone who can jump ten times his own length?"

Geraldine answered, "I know some frogs are quite good-looking. But princes are out of this world."

"They may be," said her mother, "but you can't trust them. No, you stay here with us."

Geraldine said nothing. But she did not give up her dream. Then, one day when she was tired of the jeers and the ridicule and the good advice, she told the other frogs, "I'll do it. I'll go and find a prince. Then we'll see who's laughing."

At first the others didn't believe her and they started to laugh as usual. But when Geraldine said, very firmly, "Goodbye!" and started to swim across the pond, they just stared after her, shaking their heads.

As Geraldine was halfway to the bank, doing her graceful frog-stroke, she met a pike, who eyed her in a strange way.

"Where are you off to, little frog?"

"I'm going to find a prince and marry him."

"Well, there's one in the castle not far away," said the pike. "Won't take you five minutes. So, why not rest a while with me?"

Geraldine answered politely, "No thank you, I'll be on my way."

Then the pike said, "Allow me to escort you across the water."

And he opened his mouth invitingly.

But Geraldine didn't like the look in his eye. She pushed off strongly with her hind legs and splashed across the pond, leaving the pike behind.

Safe at the other side, she sprang out onto the grass. Hop, hop, hop she went until she came to a big tree. In the branches sat a crow, who looked down at Geraldine in a strange sort of way.

"Where are you off to, little frog?"

"To the castle to marry the prince."

"I can see the castle just beyond the meadow," said the crow. "It's not far, and there's plenty of time. Why not stay here with me?"

But Geraldine answered politely, "No thank you."

So the crow said, "Would you like me to see you across the road?"

And he flew down with his beak open, invitingly.

But Geraldine didn't like the look in his eye. So she pushed off strongly with her back legs, over the green, green grass, leaving the crow behind.

Hop, hop, hop, through the hedge
at the far end of the meadow she went,
and across the road, until she came to the
high castle walls. And there she saw
a snake sunning himself.

"Where are you off to, little frog?"

"To marry the prince in the castle."

"He's just on the other side of this wall, by the side of the lake. If you follow the ditch round you'll come to a tunnel which will take you straight there. But there's no hurry, little frog, stay with me for a while."

Geraldine answered politely, “No thank you.”

So the snake said, “Would you like me to guide you round the ditch?” And he opened his mouth invitingly.

But Geraldine didn't like the look in his eye, so she pushed off strongly with her back legs. Hop, hop, hop, she went along the ditch that ran around the castle, till she found the tunnel.

Under the wall she went and came out by a lovely lake with water-lilies, bigger and grander than her own pond and swarming with fat flies and beetles. But Geraldine wasn't hungry. She swam across the water, looking for the prince.

Suddenly her legs and arms were caught. She struggled but was held fast in a net. Up she went, out of the water, into the air.

Someone was holding her, very gently, Geraldine could see him, tall, and dressed in red and gold. She knew it was the prince. She had found him at last.

Tenderly he raised her till she was close to his face. How strange he looked. Hair came out of his head and eyes, his skin was white and his mouth so small. But his voice was like music.

"Ah, ma belle. Que vous êtes jolie," he said. "How attractive you are. What a dish."

Geraldine trembled as she waited for the magic kiss.

"You look good enough to eat," he murmured.

Geraldine did not understand the caressing words, but she saw the look in his eyes. It reminded her of the pike, the crow and the snake. Then he turned and called.

"Hey, Gaston. Put the frying pan on the fire."

Geraldine gave a great slippery wriggle, shot out of his hands like a bar of soap and was in the water, swimming for dear life. Through the tunnel she went and along the ditch.

She hopped so fast the snake barely saw her as she dived through the hedge and into the meadow.

The crow saw her whizzing past and said, "Caw!"

Into the pond she leapt, swimming so strongly the pike watched her go with his mouth wide open.

By the evening she was back on her favourite lily pad, among her cousins and her aunts and uncles.

They shouted, "Didn't you find the prince, then, Geraldine?"

"But of course," she answered in a superior voice.

"And was he marvellous?" asked her mother.

"He was charming," answered Geraldine. "He even invited me to supper. But I couldn't stay."

Also available in First Young Puffin

BEAR'S BAD MOOD
John Prater

Bear is cross. His father wakes him up much too early, his favourite breakfast cereal has run out and his sisters hold a pillow-fight in his room. Even when his friends, Dog, Fox and Mole arrive, Bear just doesn't feel like playing. Instead, he runs away – and a wonderful chase begins!

GOODNIGHT, MONSTER
Carolyn Dinan

One night Dan can't get to sleep. First of all he sees a strange shadow on the wall. Then he sees huge teeth glinting and hairy feet under the bed. It couldn't really be a monster – could it?

RITA THE RESCUER
Hilda Offen

Rita Potter, the youngest of the Potter children, is a very special person. When a mystery parcel arrives at her house, Rita finds a Rescuer's outfit inside and races off to perform some very daring rescues.